Presented to

Destynee Nicole

from

Ma Ma

Date Febr 4, 2006

Dear Parents:

Everyone loves a hug! Hugs are a perfect way to send a warm message of love.

This book is very special to me because my son and I wrote it together. We talked about the times in our lives that hugs have made a wonderful difference. So cuddle up and hug your little one as you read all about hugs. We hope you enjoy our book.

Patrick Leach
Student (The apple of mom's eye.)

Sheryl Leach
Creator/Executive Producer

Art Director: Tricia Legault
Designer: June Valentine-Ruppe

ISBN 1-57064-120-X

14 15 2 3 4 5 6/0

Printed in the U.S.A.

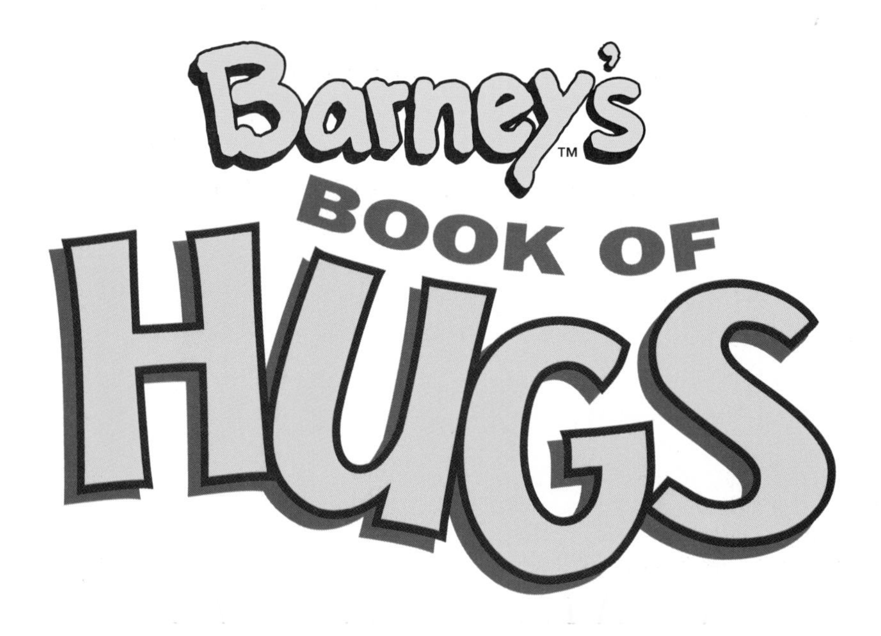

Written by
Sheryl Leach and
Patrick Leach

Illustrated by
June Valentine-Ruppe

Hugs are really simple,
Hugs are really fun.

There are many kinds of hugs.
What's your favorite one?

Barney, my favorite hug is a *birthday hug*!
A birthday hug makes me feel so special.

Or maybe . . .

My favorite hug is a *grandparent hug*.
I love it when they come to visit.

Or maybe. . .

My favorite hug is a *that's OK hug*.
Thank you. That makes me feel better.

Or maybe . . .

My favorite hug is a *puppy hug*.
Ooh! That feels all wet and tickly!

Or maybe . . .

HOME SWEET HOME
My favorite hug is a *feel better hug*.
Now it doesn't hurt so much.

Or maybe . . .

My favorite hug is a *good job hug*.
Yea! I like feeling proud.

Or maybe. . .

My favorite hug is a *don't be afraid hug*.
That makes me feel safe.

Or maybe . . .

My favorite hug is a *goodnight hug*.
Ah! Now I feel all warm and snuggly.

Or maybe. . .

My favorite hug is an *I love you hug*.
Awww. That's the best feeling of all!

To Barney
I Love you

Hugging once, hugging twice,
Every hug feels very nice.